P9-CRD-876

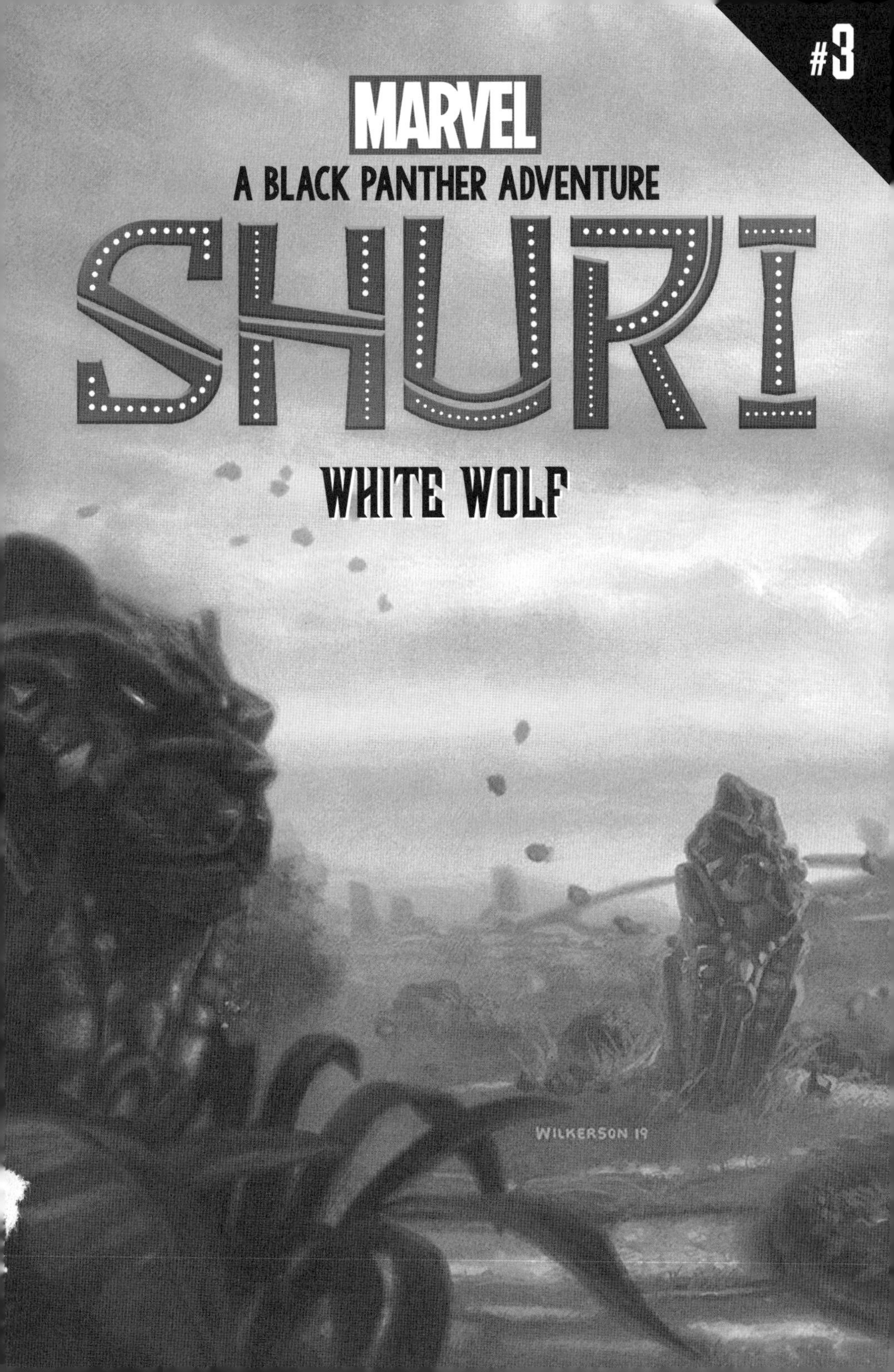
#3
MARVEL
A BLACK PANTHER ADVENTURE
SHURI
WHITE WOLF
WILKERSON 19

SHURI

BY **NIC STONE**

SCHOLASTIC INC.

Fountaindale Public Library District
300 W. Briarcliff Rd.
Bolingbrook, IL 60440

ABDOBOOKS.COM

Reinforced library bound edition published in 2021 by Spotlight, a division of ABDO, PO Box 398166, Minneapolis, Minnesota 55439. Spotlight produces high-quality reinforced library bound editions for schools and libraries. Reprinted by permission of Scholastic Inc.

Printed in the United States of America, North Mankato, Minnesota.
092020
012021

THIS BOOK CONTAINS
RECYCLED MATERIALS

© 2020 MARVEL

All rights reserved. Published by Scholastic Inc., *Publishers since 1920.* SCHOLASTIC and associated logos are trademarks and/or registered trademarks of Scholastic Inc.

The publisher does not have any control over and does not assume any responsibility for author or third-party websites or their content.

No part of this publication may be reproduced, stored in a retrieval system, or transmitted in any form or by any means, electronic, mechanical, photocopying, recording, or otherwise, without written permission of the publisher. For information regarding permission, write to Scholastic Inc., Attention: Permissions Department, 557 Broadway, New York, NY 10012.

This book is a work of fiction. Names, characters, places, and incidents are either the product of the author's imagination or are used fictitiously, and any resemblance to actual persons, living or dead, business establishments, events, or locales is entirely coincidental.

First printing 2020

Book design by Katie Fitch

Library of Congress Control Number: 2020942440

Publisher's Cataloging-in-Publication Data

Names: Stone, Nic, author.
Title: White wolf / by Nic Stone
Description: Minneapolis, Minnesota : Spotlight, 2021. | Series: Shuri: a Black Panther adventure; #3
Summary: Storm accompanies Shuri and K'Marah to their next destination to meet White Wolf, but their trip uncovers a cosmic solution to the dying plants, a strange sickness, and a threat to Wakanda.
Identifiers: ISBN 9781532147753 (lib. bdg.)
Subjects: LCSH: Shuri (Fictitious character)--Juvenile fiction. | Wakanda (Africa : Imaginary place)--Juvenile fiction. | Princesses--Juvenile fiction. | Plants--Juvenile fiction. | Diseases--Juvenile fiction. | Adventure and adventurers--Juvenile fiction. | Black Panther (Fictitious character)--Juvenile fiction | Graphic novels--Juvenile fiction
Classification: DDC [Fic]--dc23

Spotlight
A Division of ABDO
abdobooks.com

FOR KALANI JOY AND ALL THE LITTLE BROWN-SKINNED
SUPER-GENIUSES. STEAM ON, LOVES.
—NIC

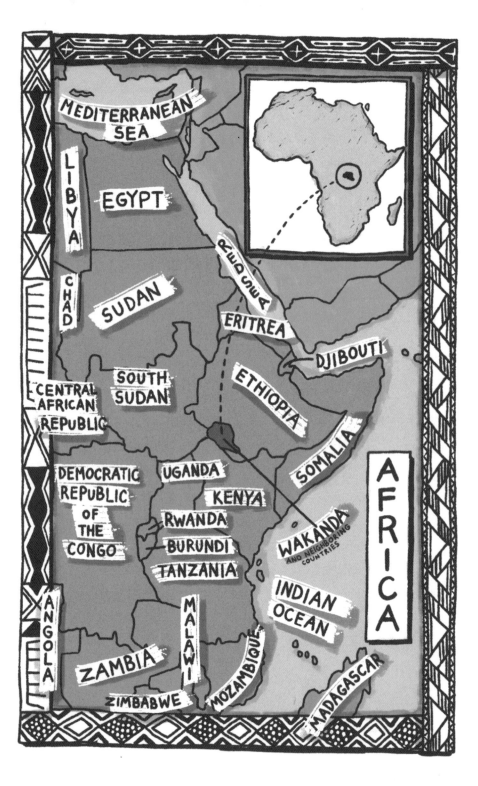

12

INTEL

Ororo *does* know of someone.

But.

"I hate to be the source of disappointment for a *second* time, Princess Shuri, but I'm not entirely sure I could even *get* to the person I'm thinking of," Ororo says sadly. "He's . . . detained at present."

"Detained . . . ?"

Ororo looks back and forth between the girls and sighs. "Is there something happening in Wakanda, Shuri? I understand your concern for saving your herb, and I want to be of service, but I need to know what I am walking into, and—not to discredit your very valid concerns—whether or not sharing highly confidential information with you is worth the risk."

Now Shuri is nervous.

"What I understand from what your brother shared with me years ago, this herb is a vital component of the Black Panther mantle, yes?"

Shuri nods. "In order to fully become the Black Panther, an individual must ingest the herb. It enhances speed, strength, agility, and kinesthetic sensory processing. Makes a man . . ." *or woman*, she thinks, "into a giant cat while simultaneously augmenting the advanced cognitive capabilities we already possess as members of the *Homo sapiens* species."

"Maybe *I* should eat a leaf or two . . ." K'Marah says.

"You'd die," Shuri replies.

Ororo draws back. "Well, that's a bit harsh."

"Yeah, seriously!" K'Marah says. "I was kidding!"

"Well, I wasn't." Shuri focuses her attention back on Ororo. "Anyone who eats of the herb unworthily won't survive it."

"Huh," Ororo says. "I guess that makes sense. I'm sure it prevents would-be megalomaniacs from finding and eating it and becoming instantly powerful. Not that Wakanda *has* any citizens like that." She grins. "How often does a sitting Black Panther have to take it to maintain its effects?"

"Uhh, as far as we know, only once."

"So . . . and forgive me if this question seems dense," Ororo says (and Shuri knows they're about to head downhill), "but if the Black Panther never has to ingest it again, why the urgency to save it *now*?"

Shuri sighs. *Why are grown-ups so thickheaded sometimes?*

"The ritual Challenge Day is coming. That's the day when—"

"—any number of self-selected opponents can challenge T'Challa to a bout of hand-to-hand combat for the throne. I'm familiar."

"Right. Well, at the current rate, the herb will die out completely on the day of the Challenge. So if T'Challa loses—though I don't believe he will," she adds for good measure, "the *new* king and Black Panther will be nothing more than a regular dude who happened to kick T'Challa's butt. This might be fine *within* Wakanda—provided no one decides to run a coup and overtake the throne by force. But what if forces attack from outside?" Shuri says. "What happens if the enhanced abilities of the Black Panther are needed, but unobtainable?"

"And then there's *you*," K'Marah says, jumping in.

Which makes Shuri's already-racing heart leap up into her skull so she can *hear* just how nervous she is. "What do you mean?"

"I mean, I don't know what *your* future plans are, but *I* certainly hope that you'll one day become queen and Black Panther—*Pantheress*, really." She stretches out a hand to look at her fingernails. "It's the only reason I'm training to become a Dora Milaje. So I can go kick butt with you."

A new light flickers on inside Shuri. "K'Marah, that might be the kindest thing you've ever said to me."

"Well, don't get too excited." K'Marah yawns. "If you don't figure out how to save the herbal thingy, no Pantheress action for *you*. I guess T'Challa can keep being Panther once you're queen since he'll allegedly still have the juice in his veins. But not even he will be able to fight forever."

Ororo sighs again. Her gaze drifts out the window, and Shuri sees a flash of lightning in the distance. Had "Ororo Storm" done that just now? Are random lightning strikes a part of *her* thinking face?

"Okay," she says, turning back to Shuri. "I will tell you this, but understand up front that *I* cannot get you access to this person. But knowing you, I'm sure you'll find a way."

Shuri accidentally kicks K'Marah beneath the table in excitement.

"OW!"

"Sorry!" the princess says.

Ororo shakes her head. "Your brother is going to put a price on my head," she says more to the air than to Shuri. "Steve Rogers will, too, if he finds out I shared this intel with a pair of eighth graders."

K'Marah's eyes go wide and she leans in to whisper to Shuri: "Is she talking about *Captain Americ—*"

"Hush, K'Marah!"

Ororo continues: "There is a man named Dr. Erik Selvig who is an expert in . . . cosmically derived paraphernalia, we'll call it. I would be stunned if he *didn't* know all about Vibranium. I'm almost sure he could give you more information about it than anyone else on Earth could."

Barring my father's murderer . . . The thought pops into Shuri's mind unbidden, and she does her best to shake it away. The one person she would never actively seek out is the man who took her and T'Challa's father away, not only from them, but from every citizen of Wakanda.

"The *access* issue, though, is twofold. One: Everyone believes him to be dead. Which means you can't just ask around for how to get to him. Two: From what

I understand, he's a bit . . . unhinged. Steve—Captain America—saved him for reasons he hasn't disclosed, but know that even if you manage to get to him, there's a chance he won't have anything useful to say."

But Shuri has to try, anyway, doesn't she? "Do you know where this man is being held, Ororo?"

The older woman looks right into Shuri's eyes. There's a steadfastness there that Shuri hopes to one day emulate. "He's in London."

A gasp of delighted surprise escapes the princess's lips. "London?"

Ororo gives her a single nod of confirmation. "Correct."

"YES!" And the princess is on her feet with her fist in the air. "K'Marah, we're going to London!"

"Now just a minute, Shuri," Ororo says, rising to *her* feet. "What I will *not* do is permit you two to leave my care on a wild goose chase in a city where you have no contacts—"

"But we *do* have a contact in London!" Shuri exclaims. "There was an entire Hatut Zeraze base there!"

"*Hatut Zeraze* . . ." K'Marah rolls the phrase around on her tongue. "Dogs of War . . . Wait! The Dogs of War are *real?*" she exclaims. "I thought they were urban legend!"

Which doesn't surprise Shuri in the least. Before T'Challa disbanded the group upon his ascent to the throne, there were members of Wakanda's most elite group of spies (and assassins, though Shuri tries not to think about that part) stationed across the globe. Their existence was kept so tightly under wraps, however, most Wakandans believed the Dogs of War to be little more than modern myth. An unconfirmed watchful eye whispered to keep enemies—and disobedient children— on their toes. "They're technically not active anymore, but they were as real as the beads on your braids," Shuri replies. "Though you're not supposed to know that, so shh!" She shakes a finger at K'Marah, then turns back to Ororo. "I'll just touch base with the contact in London, then we'll be out of your rather glorious hair."

"No," Ororo says.

"No?"

"No. Not to go all 'big sis' on you, but I won't allow you two to leave *this* country until I have spoken with an *adult* at your destination."

"But I—"

At the literal lightning flash of *try-me-if-you-want-to* in Ororo's eyes, Shuri's shoulders slump in surrender.

"Yes, ma'am," she says. "We'll have to return to my transport vessel to make contact, though." Shuri lifts the arm with her Kimoyo bracelet to eye level and taps a bead. The words *No Service* illuminate in an arc above her palm.

K'Marah falls asleep almost as soon as the door of the Jeep is shut, so they ride in silence for the first few minutes of the journey back to the plain where the *Predator* is parked, this time with Ororo sitting "shotgun," as Shuri's heard it called.

But a kilometer or so outside the town proper, the weather-wielding woman rotates in her seat and levels the princess with one of her signature (read: abject terror-inducing) narrowed-eye glares. "Who, exactly, are you planning to contact, *Dada*?"

Shuri feels Ororo's sudden suspicion pass over her like a heat wave.

In truth, the princess is surprised it took her this long to ask. Shuri is certain that Ororo, as T'Challa's first flame, previous pen pal, and present greatest ally, knows more about Wakanda's government and intelligence networks than even *she* does. Surely Ororo Munroe is aware of which Hatut Zeraze were stationed in London—she should know exactly whom Shuri intends to reach out to.

She's even met him. He was still in Wakanda back when Ororo and T'Challa were getting acquainted.

"Well . . ." Shuri says. "Not that T'Challa would approve, but . . ."

Based on Ororo's expression *now*, Shuri would say she's finally caught on.

"You're not serious, Shuri. *Him?* Really? Not only will T'Challa not 'approve,' he'll short-circuit!"

"Which is why we aren't going to tell him," Shuri replies.

Ororo just shakes her head. "I guess on the bright side, if anyone can get you to Dr. Selvig, it's him."

"Right?" Shuri says, her excitement building. "That's what I was thinking. He knows everyone."

They lapse back into quiet, and the air around their moving vehicle seems to crackle.

"Shuri?" Ororo says.

"Yes?"

"I'm coming with you."

MISSION LOG

IT'S A GOOD THING ORORO DECIDED TO
ACCOMPANY US: IN MY EXCITEMENT ABOUT
HAVING A CLEAR PATH TO THE NEXT LEAD, I
NEGLECTED TO CONSIDER THE GREAT DISTANCE
BETWEEN HAIPO AND LONDON, AND THE TIME
IT WOULD TAKE TO MAKE THE JOURNEY.

At top speed, the *Predator* (and fine:
The name has grown on me) should've been
able to cover the 7,237-kilometer distance in just under three hours. But
since I didn't get an opportunity to *test*
"flight at that speed with this precise
amount of weight," as Ororo put it, we're
flying at 75 percent of the maximum velocity, and with the time change, will arrive
ninety-three minutes before sunset.

Which means there's a good chance we'll be staying overnight.

And losing more time.

T'Challa didn't blow a gasket and decide to send our entire Air Force after me like I expected him to, and he *did* agree to stay mum about our little trek and cover for us so Mother won't come after me, either. If I had to guess, I'd say it's because Ororo was standing beside me, smiling and batting her silvery eyelashes, when I made the call.

I told him about the outpost K'Marah and I saw as we left—though he didn't seem too concerned or alarmed. Not entirely sure what to think of that, but at any rate, our contact is expecting us and has been briefed on the purpose of our visit.

All that to say: Everything is in order, and I should be able to recline in my impeccably ergonomically designed, shock-absorbent captain's chair and enjoy our smooth, invisible flight . . .

But I can't. The Challenge is in just over two days, and with each minute that ticks by, my wariness grows.

Something odd: When we returned to the *Predator*—which had been in Invisi-mode the entire time it sat on the plain just outside Haipo—there was a new security image. It was the same sunglasses and kufi-wearing man as before, but in this image, he didn't seem to be looking *up* as much as straight ahead—right into the camera. What's more, it seems this new photo was captured at a much closer distance than the previous one.

I'm not entirely sure what to make of it. I've checked both the software and the security mechanism itself to see if there might be a glitch that would result in the delayed processing or delivery of a captured image, but all appeared to be in working order. It's possible that there was a network issue in flight that deferred the upload . . .

Or there's someone who can, not only see the vessel while it's "invisible," but also managed to follow us to Kenya. (Which is totally and completely improbable. Isn't it?)

Trying not to think *too* much about it. Especially with so many other moving parts.

So. New objectives:

- Get to the White Wolf.
- Get the White Wolf to get me to Dr. Selvig.
- Very quickly gather all the very helpful information Dr. Selvig has stored away in his brain just *waiting* to be set free.
- Return Ororo to Haipo and get back to Wakanda as quickly as possible (without her being all *Safety first!* I think we'll be able to fly at closer to 90 percent of maximum velocity).
- Save the herb, and by extension, the country.

Because this is the way things *have* to go.
There are no other options.

Oh! A note: Ororo's X-(Wo)Man stretchy—and moisture-wicking—Storm suit is made of something called polyelastane. I shall begin Vibranium-infusion trials as soon as I manage to acquire a bolt of the fabric.

13

WHITE WOLF

Shuri is just dozing off when the alarm begins to blare. She bolts upright and a sharp pain shoots across the center of her back—might need to reexamine the "impeccable" ergonomics of her captain's chair—but it's nothing compared to the ringing in her ears.

"What is it?" K'Marah shouts, also jolted from her sleep by the shrieking noise. "What's happening?"

"I'm . . . I'm not sure," the princess replies.

What she *is* sure of? She must stay calm.

Thoughts of Baba and predawn mornings spent "meditating" (read: wriggling at his side while *he* meditated) fill her head. "You must maintain your center at all times, child," he used to say in a voice that rang like the deeply resonant music of an upright bass. "Tether yourself to that which is unshakable: the glory and endurance of our great nation."

Shuri takes a steadying breath and attempts to do just that when her Kimoyo bracelet and card begin to vibrate almost simultaneously.

Mother on one, and T'Challa on the other.

A glance around at the cockpit meters and gauges reveals consistent altitude and air pressure within the cabin, and it hits her: The alarm she's hearing is the one she connected to her homeland's nationwide emergency alert system.

Something terrible is happening in Wakanda.

"Oh no," she hears K'Marah say behind her. "Grandmother is calling . . ."

"I think there's something going on back home—"

"SHURI, WHERE ARE YOU?" A hologram of Queen Ramonda leaps up from Shuri's now-illuminated Kimoyo card, and the princess stumbles back. "Mother! I—"

But there's a thump and shout, and the queen gasps and turns to look at something on her right that Shuri can't see before the Kimoyo call drops and her likeness vanishes.

"Mother!" Shuri grabs for the device, but then—

"Sist—you must retur—"

"T'Challa!" Shuri scrambles over to the vessel's radio, thankful she took Ororo's advice and gave him the frequency information when they last spoke, "in case of an emergency that requires the use of more *vintage* technology." "T'Challa, what's going on?"

"—breach at the wester—"

But he keeps breaking up. "Brother?"

"—vasion! Enter at the northea—"

There's a burst of static, and he cuts out entirely.

"T'Challa? T'Challa!"

"Can we turn the alarm *off?*" K'Marah has appeared at Shuri's shoulder with her hands over her ears. "I can't hear myself think!"

"Where is Ororo?" Shuri asks, squatting down to disconnect the alarm sensor from the *Predator*'s speaker system. "We need to reroute."

The interior of the cabin goes suddenly silent, and when Shuri looks up, K'Marah is gazing down at her friend with her head cocked and mouth turned down. "Who?" she says.

"Ororo Munroe, aka *Storm*, aka Mistress of the Elements, aka your personal heroine? Where is she?"

"I have no idea what you're talking about, Shuri."

"This isn't the time for *jokes*, K'Marah," Shuri says, pushing past her friend. "Our country is being *invaded*, and we need to get back to it. Ororo?" she shouts, knocking on the small lavatory door. "Are you in there?"

"There is no Ororo here, Shuri," says a voice from where K'Marah was standing . . .

But it no longer sounds like K'Marah.

Shuri's pulse roars in her ears as blood rushes to her head.

Because she *knows* that voice.

She shuts her eyes and inhales deeply to steady herself—and then she turns.

The woman from her vision is standing between the chairs in the *Predator*'s open cockpit.

"There is no one here to save you, Princess." Puffs of dust leave the woman's mouth with each word, and when she smiles, the cracks in her skin deepen, and a few desiccated chunks drop from her face. "There is no one here to save *you*, and *you* failed to save your country—"

"NO!" Shuri surges toward her, but the woman shoves a hand forward, and the princess is thrown back against the far wall by a grit-filled wind that scorches her skin.

She cries out in pain and tries to get back on her feet.

Another wind hits her, and she inhales what feels like little pieces of burning coal. She coughs. Gags.

"Shuri—"

"*Khusela, khusela . . .*" The voices from the fire ring through Shuri's mind.

The woman is standing over her now. She doesn't want to give up, but what choice does she have? A fissured hand reaches toward her face, but to her surprise, the touch against her cheek is blissfully cool. Her eyelids begin to droop.

"*Shuri . . .*"

"No . . ." The princess whispers, sinking farther into the heat surrounding her. Everything burns. Except for her cheek . . .

"*SHURI! DADA!*"

"No . . ." The faintest whisper now.

"Shuri, you must wake!"

There's a booming crack of thunder, and Shuri sits up.

"Are you okay, sweetheart?" Ororo says, placing a cool hand on her face. "You're very warm."

Shuri stares into Ororo's blue eyes—searching for a tether—but doesn't speak.

"You were having a dream," Ororo continues. "A bad one from the looks of it. Are you all right?"

A dream.

Before she realizes it's coming, Shuri's cheeks are warm and wet.

"Oh dear." Ororo kneels before the princess and takes her hands. She opens her mouth to speak but then . . . just smiles. "You know, this is exactly what your brother was doing when I met *him*."

The stories float to the front of Shuri's mind. T'Challa claims *he* saved *Ororo* from being kidnapped by a white man on a rainy night in the jungle, but Ororo claims *she* saved *T'Challa* from being kidnapped by a group of white men on a Kenyan plain beneath a clear, blue sky.

She peeks over her shoulder. K'Marah, still not feeling well, is curled up beneath one of the Vibranium core–weighted blankets Shuri created for those nights when she couldn't get her brain to stop spinning. With the gentle weight and the sound absorption, she'd sleep like a newborn underneath it—sort of like her friend is doing now.

Should Shuri tell Ororo about the vision at the bonfire? About the nightmare she just had? The weather goddess *is* probably Wakanda's greatest ally out in the wider world.

"I—" Shuri begins, but then there's a ringing noise from just above the radar. *"Warning: This vessel has been detected."*

And back to reality. "Are we not in Invisi-mode?" Shuri says, leaping to her feet to check the flight instruments. They're flying over the English Channel, still a hundred and seventy kilometers or so south of London . . .

The cloaking mechanism is turned up to 100 percent.

Shuri huffs and shakes her head. "There must be a glitch. I tested the stealth tech numerous times, including multiple trips over the marketplace at peak hours, and even a veritable *spy* excursion when I followed T'Challa on one of his surveillance runs around the borders. At no point was I 'detected'—"

Letters and numbers begin to appear on the screen of the *Predator*'s GPS. "What th—"

But then Shuri *and* Ororo are thrown sideways as the aircraft suddenly course corrects.

"Shuri!" Ororo says, trying to prevent the princess from falling. They both collide with the side wall.

"I'm not sure what's happening," Shuri says, doing her best to stay calm. She looks at the aircraft control panel. "How is—"

"*Sorry to intrude.*" A gruff male voice fills the air from the staticky radio.

Which just reminds her of that stupid dream.

"Is everything all right?" K'Marah suddenly says from the back.

Shuri and Ororo both turn to her, and then to each other.

"Wellll . . ." the princess says.

K'Marah, of course, notices their trepidation. "Oh no. Are we losing altitude and on course to crash into the sea in an explosion of watery glory?"

"This aircraft will be remotely directed to a secure location," the staticky voice goes on. "Any attempts to interfere and/or regain control of the vessel will result in immediate engine failure—"

No one on board breathes as what sounds like a scuffle ensues on the other end of the radio. Voices—at least two, and both gravelly and masculine—cut in and out, but Shuri picks up on little blips like "*idiot . . .*" and "*scare the . . .*" and "*protocol*" and "*gimme that . . .*"

Then a voice Shuri *does* recognize (Ororo recognizes it, too, if the roll of her eyes is any indication) crackles through the small speaker: "*Baby sis? That you? We can't see or hear your approach, but there's an odd winged cat–shaped mass of Vibranium crossing into UK airspace from the south . . .*"

Now Shuri smiles and exhales. Of course a group of Wakandans would have the tools and technology to detect Vibranium in the atmosphere, even twenty-eight thousand feet up.

"'Baby sis'?" K'Marah looks more baffled than if someone had told her the Dora Milaje will now be run by men.

"Oh brother," Ororo says, staring at the radio speaker and shaking her head.

Brother, indeed. "K'Marah, you're about to meet my adopted big bro, Hunter."

"Hunter?" K'Marah says.

"I can't believe I'm letting you do this," from Ororo.

"Yes, Hunter," Shuri continues, ignoring Ororo. "Formerly known as the White Wolf."

14

SPACE CADET

In its descent, the *Predator* passes over the bustling city of London, and the girls marvel as Ororo points out things they've only ever read about in their digital European history textbooks: the River Thames and Tower Bridge and Westminster Abbey and Buckingham Palace. There's even a building shaped like a space capsule and what appears to be a giant Ferris wheel—the *London Eye*, Ororo says it's called.

After another three or four minutes, the vessel approaches what appears to be the warehouse portion of an industrial district, and they slow to a near-stop above a cluster of nondescript brick buildings.

Shuri glances at the control panel right as the *Predator* switches into hover mode.

"Whoa!" K'Marah says from her post next to one of the vessel's one-way glass side windows. "Shuri, come look!"

The girls watch in stunned silence as the roof of a building to their right splits down the center and slides open, revealing a landing pad with a white target painted at its center.

The radio crackles again, just about scaring both girls—*and* Ororo—out of their skins. "Seat belts!" Hunter's voice says. "It's windy down here. Landing might be a little turbulent."

And turbulent it is. In fact, by the time they touch down within the building and the roof begins to slide shut above them, Shuri is so nauseated, she can barely move.

She hears the vessel's belly hatch yawn open, and the rhythmic *thu-thunk* of thick heels as someone comes on board. Then a woman she's never seen before appears over her right shoulder. She has something shiny and black draped over her forearm, and is carrying a silver tray topped with three half-filled glasses of bubbly brown liquid. "Princess Shuri," she says with a reverent nod of her head and slight bow. "Honored to have you with us. The polyelastane you requested." She lifts her elbow slightly and gestures with her head to the length of what Shuri realizes is fabric.

The princess slides it off her arm. "Thank you," she says as she takes the woman in. She has beautiful umber skin and an angular face, with extremely close-cropped blond hair. And she's wearing an olive-colored jumpsuit—lots of pockets—and brown lace-up boots.

As Shuri's eyes trail back up the woman's tall frame, they stick on a patch sewn onto her left shoulder: three horizontal stripes, green at the top and bottom, red in the middle, with a centralized image of a red panther against a black circle.

The flag of Wakanda.

"I am Lena," the woman says. "I will be the point of contact for the duration of your stay in London." She hands each of them a glass. "Drink up."

"What is it?" K'Marah says warily, her Dora training actually kicking into gear for once.

It makes Lena smile. "Ginger ale. To settle your stomachs. I wanted to fly you *around* that pocket of bumpy air, but Hunter insisted we pull you through it." She leans forward conspiratorially and lowers her voice. "Feel free to thank him by vomiting on his alligator shoes."

Within minutes, Lena is collecting their empty glasses—the beverage did, in fact, help *easy the queasy*, as K'Marah so aptly puts it—and then they're following her out the aircraft and toward a wide steel door Shuri wouldn't have noticed had she not been looking right at it. As they advance, an iris scanner folds down from the wall, and Lena leans in. "I have heard much of your brilliance, Princess, so you'll have to excuse our humble base of operations," she says as a purple laser, not unlike the one on Shuri's palm scanner, flashes over her eyeball. "Our faction's shift from offensive to observational has . . . taken some getting used to."

Ororo snorts. "I bet."

"At any rate, Hunter is excited to see you." The door opens, and the pair of girls and pair of women step through.

While Shuri doesn't know all the details of Hatut Zeraze's disbandment, she does know that the secret police was created by her father during his reign as king. He'd appointed his adopted son, Hunter, as the leader.

Shuri also knows T'Challa decommissioned the Hatut Zeraze shortly after ascending to the throne . . . and that he and Hunter have never really gotten along.

Years prior to T'Challa's birth, Hunter was taken in by King T'Chaka after a plane crash on Wakandan land killed Hunter's birth family. Shuri suspects that Hunter resents T'Challa for . . . being born, really: As the birth son, it made T'Challa the rightful heir to the Wakandan throne. She also has a hunch that T'Challa, *despite* being the true heir, resented being in Hunter's shadow—she's heard the White Wolf constantly out-performed T'Challa when they were young.

Hunter had left Wakanda on assignment by the time Shuri was born, and she's technically only met him in person twice: first at Baba's funeral, and second at T'Challa's coronation after he bested S'Yan to become king. And she's heard rumors of his brutality.

But he's always been nice to her.

"Second doorway on the left," Lena says, stepping aside so Shuri can walk ahead of her up the bare hallway with dingy tile floors and those terrible fluorescent lights buzzing in the ceiling. "He's waiting for you, so go right in."

The princess's palms dampen as the weight of this impromptu visit settles on her head like a crown of plutonium. What leads will she have if Hunter can't get her to this Selvig fellow? What will she do? All of this time spent getting here and then—

"Well, if it isn't my beautiful baby sister! My, how you've grown!" says the green-eyed man rising from behind a wide desk as Shuri and the others step into the modestly furnished room. He's around T'Challa's height and of a similar build, but bearded and with slick, dark hair that's pulled into a knot on top of his head.

And also: He's . . . not brown.

"*That* is Hunter?" K'Marah says, too stunned to keep her voice down. "But he has the complexion of a *colonizer*!"

Shuri feels her face heat, but the Caucasian man just laughs. "You're very observant," he says with a wink. "Guess you can see why they call me the 'White Wolf.'"

Storm disappears on some intel-acquiring mission for the X-Men, and the princess spends the evening refining the small bit of raw Vibranium she has on board the *Predator* for emergencies, and works at getting it to bind with the polyelastane fabric.

To her great relief, by morning, Hunter has not only managed to locate Dr. Selvig, he also "called in a few favors" (the coldness with which he says the phrase makes Shuri's peace-loving flesh crawl, but she soldiers on) and arranged for Shuri to have ten minutes with him.

And it's a good thing she took K'Marah's "ridiculous" advice and brought her dress: Her cover will involve a brief appearance as a foreign biotechnology student at a benefit gala hosted by the local university where Dr. Selvig is hidden away in an underground laboratory.

"Just be ready to smile and nod," Lena tells her as they move throughout the city making "preparations."

K'Marah, who claims she's been "backhanded by a wave of nausea-inducing jet lag or something," hangs back at the outpost while Lena takes Shuri to a Ghanaian spa in the city to be scrubbed and polished, and with as much as the princess has on her mind, the day blurs by. One minute, she's trying not to squirm while a woman scrubs her feet, and the next, she's back at the outpost—hair, nails, and makeup done (she can wipe off the face but is fully aware that Mother will ask questions about the mani-pedi) and smelling of amber, iris, and patchouli—with Lena helping her into her dress.

Speaking of Lena, she and the two Wakandan men who will accompany them to meet Hunter are all wearing sleek black tuxedos. They're also traveling in a large luxury vehicle she heard someone refer to by the name of another cat of prey: the jaguar.

She hates to admit it considering the circumstances, but for the first time in her life, the princess of Wakanda feels quite fancy. Less a dolled-up bauble made to hang at the queen's side, and more glamorous and important in her own right. The feeling fuels her: Surely T'Challa gets to feel this way all the time.

Stepping into the gala space is jarring: The princess has never seen so many pale-skinned people in one place. With everyone in their fancy clothes, it's like moving through a sea of colored, crystal-studded snow.

Shuri doesn't know the backstory details that have spread about her, but as she crosses the room to meet Hunter in a side hallway as planned, more than a few people stop her to make strange comments about how "impressed" they are that a girl "like *you*" or "where *you're* from" has been "able to accomplish so much." One older Caucasian couple holds her fast for three solid minutes to discuss how "glad" they are she "made it out of the bastion of corruption and poverty that is sub-Saharan Africa."

Shuri finally escapes the crowd, and as she and Hunter take one hallway and staircase after another, her mind spins through the bizarre experience. It's clear that many of the gala attendees hold similar ideas, not only about whatever country she's supposedly from, but about the entire continent. Which seems . . . silly to the princess. What would *these* people think if they knew about Wakanda? Would they even believe it to be real?

Shuri's never been so relieved to exit a too-bright space and step into a darker one.

Because Dr. Erik Selvig's lab is just that: dark.

"We must keep the light low so they don't think we have the cube," he says nonsensically as Shuri and Hunter enter the room. A balding white man in full lab regalia—black slacks, button-down, tie, white coat—scurries around the bizarrely furnished room. There are strange machines scattered about, each with random-looking buttons and dials, the likes of which Shuri has never seen. He bounces between them muttering what sounds to the princess like gibberish under his breath: something about a red skull and a "hydra" and "Kobik." The only thing Shuri *does* recognize is the name "Captain America."

"Dr. Selvig, you have a guest," says the squirrelly man who escorted them through a series of high-security doors to reach the lab.

"A guest?" Selvig replies, startled. "Did they bring the cube? I don't want the cube." And he puts his hands up in surrender before beginning to mumble and pace again.

Shuri jumps right in: "Sir, do you know anything about Vibranium?"

"Which type?" the man says without missing a beat.

At this, Shuri turns to Hunter, not sure she heard the man correctly. Hunter just shrugs.

"There is only one type, sir—"

"Incorrect."

"Huh?"

"There are two known types of Vibranium: Antarctic, the location of which is self-explanatory, and Wakandan, found only in the insular East African nation known as the Wakandas."

The princess tries not to take offense at the word *insular*.

She also wonders if there really is a supply of Vibranium in Antarctica. The notion seems absurd based on what she's been taught her whole life: Vibranium was a gift from Bast and Wakanda is the only nation on Earth with access to it.

But a lot of what she thought she knew has been upended—it's why she's here. Really, is it that far-fetched an idea?

She sets it on a back burner for now. "I mean the type found in Wakanda—"

"Is that where you're from?" The scientist whips around, and Shuri takes a step backward despite there already being a significant amount of distance between them.

She decides to ignore the question—just in case. "Say there was a plant whose cells became infused with Wakandan Vibranium."

His eyes narrow as his gaze shifts to a point somewhere above Shuri's head. "It is feasible, yes."

"Based on what *you* know of Wakandan Vibranium, would a change in the climate or the soil cause that plant to die?"

"Has the plant been moved?" He returns to one of his machines and fiddles with a few dials.

"No, sir," Shuri replies.

"Then no. I have studied both forms of Vibranium—there is an amount of the Wakandan variety in Captain America's shield, in fact—and nothing organic in the earthly sense could disintegrate Vibranium bonds with any other cells. Additionally, the Vibranium itself would cause the plant to be highly adaptable to changes in climate and natural shifts in soil pH," he says.

Shuri deflates. "Okay," she says, trying to keep her voice level. "So what could cause Vibranium-infused organic matter to shrivel and die?"

Now he turns to her and smiles. Which makes her want to leap from her own skin. "Well, Princess," he says, and Hunter steps forward.

"Watch it, old man."

How does he know who I am? Shuri thinks.

Selvig waves the brutish man off and rotates on a heel to begin pacing again. "The only thing that could disrupt Vibranium bonds with organic matter—like plant cells—would be a foreign agent. A poison—"

"But I checked the cells—"

He holds up a hand and Shuri's mouth snaps shut. "A *poison* in the sense of a substance that causes illness or death in living organisms, but one not typically found in nature," he goes on. "Which would mean one of two things." He stops moving and stands up straight with his hands behind his back. "Has there been any abnormal celestial activity over the Wakandas as of late?"

"I don't think so," Shuri says.

"Correct!" Selvig's finger shoots into the air. "The most recent celestial disturbance was over the city of Chicago two nights ago, in fact."

This guy is so weird, Shuri thinks. "Okay . . ."

"So there's your answer. You may go."

Baffled, the princess actually looks around. "Huh?"

"You're dealing with a *mutated* substance." He whips around and looks at her like *Duh, you dummy.*

"Uhhh . . . all right. So this substance is undetectable at the molecular level?"

"None of that matters," he says before his eyes alight on an instrument to Shuri and Hunter's right. He races over to check it. "Your plants aren't dying naturally, and you need to change your question. It's not *what* is killing them. It's *who*."

15

DETECTED

Shuri's mind is reeling as she and Hunter ascend what feel like eight billion steps to get back to ground level from Dr. Selvig's laboratory. Hunter's contact—the squirrelly guy who flinches every time the White Wolf *blinks* in his direction—leads them down a hall away from the festivities in the grand ballroom, and soon the cool night air is hitting Shuri's face.

Could what Dr. Selvig suggested be true? Is there someone *inside* Wakanda deliberately poisoning the heart-shaped herb? Shuri hates to admit it, but the whole way up from the lab, all she could think about was Ororo. Not because the princess thinks *she's* poisoning the herb . . . but because "who" and "mutated" make Shuri think of mutants. (*Is that discrimination?* she wonders.)

Are there any mutants inside Wakanda? That would make them Wakandan mutants. The thought of which is jarring, but . . . well, why wouldn't there be?

But also: Why would a Wakandan want to kill the heart-shaped herb?

The princess is silent for the entire drive back to the outpost, and though she catches Lena eyeing her with concern more than once, Shuri is thankful when the woman doesn't ask any questions.

A call comes in mere minutes before they reach their destination, and it's clear from the wary looks and hushed exchange of whispers that the trio of Wakandan (former?) secret agents is being called to a mission that doesn't involve babysitting a pair of tween rogues.

Once they've pulled the car into an underground garage at the back of the building, Lena turns to Shuri. "Princess, we must attend to some business in the city, but you and your travel companions will be safe here. I will escort you upstairs—"

"That's okay. Just tell me which floor, and you all can go."

Lena opens her mouth—surely to rebut—but then closes it and nods. "Very well, Your Majesty," she says, removing a single bead from her Kimoyo bracelet. "You will need to hold this up to the security scanner within the elevator. Fourth floor. A room has been prepared for you next door to your friend, whom I believe is resting still. You're the third door on the left. Ororo requested quarters with roof access, so she's one floor up at the opposite end of the long hallway."

"Okay. Thank you, Lena." Shuri moves to exit the vehicle.

But Lena's hand lands on her arm. "Are you sure you're all right, Shuri?" she says, face ablaze with what Shuri can only describe as *readiness to throw down.*

It makes the princess feel safer than she has in quite a long while. Which impels her to tell the truth: "To be honest, Lena, I'm not." Shuri turns to her and smiles. "But I will be."

They all watch as Shuri steps into the elevator, and she waves as the doors slide shut.

But she doesn't press the button for the fourth floor. Because right now, Shuri's mind is whirring like a centrifuge, trying to separate what she knows for sure from that which she can only speculate about.

When she gets like this at home, the princess either fidgets with something or takes a long walk. Since it's a delightfully cool night and she doesn't have enough raw Vibranium or the tools she needs to refine it in order to begin the infusion trials on the polyelastane fabric, she chooses the latter, holding the DOORS CLOSE button on the elevator panel for a stretch of a few minutes.

Once she's sure her overseers have had adequate time to not only leave but also return in case something was forgotten, she lets go of the button and stands to the side as the doors reopen. Then she peeks out . . . and releases a head-clearing sigh of relief when she sees that the coast is clear.

She was right about the area they're in: It's full of warehouses and three- to five-story industrial buildings. From the front, she can see that the building they're in—which Hunter let slip is Wakandan-owned—is much larger than she realized. She knew it was five floors high but had no idea it encompassed an entire block.

Which just sets Shuri's brain to spinning again. Where else in the world are there Wakandans stationed? The princess met three emissaries from her homeland in addition to her adopted brother, but with a building this size, there have to be *more* people working here. She wonders how many.

Are there outposts like this in major cities across the globe? Shuri finds the thought staggering—even more so than the notion of T'Challa revealing their existence to everyone. It makes a series of doubts burble in her stomach: There's obviously much more to being a ruler than she realized. Does she even have what it takes?

The past few days flood back over Shuri: from the failed suit trials to the Taifa Ngao and first mention of the word *invasion*. From the bonfire and vision, to the discovery of the dying herbs. From seeing T'Challa and Okoye with the war council to her and K'Marah's bizarre exit from Wakanda. From the overwhelming heat in Kenya to meeting Dr. Selvig.

A breeze rustles some debris just over the edge of the curb, and Shuri realizes how cool it's gotten. Is midsummer in London always this nippy at night?

The princess rubs her skinny arms and picks up speed. What she *should* do is return to the outpost, wake K'Marah, and get them en route back home. She's wasted enough time away: The Challenge is *tomorrow*, and though she hasn't exactly solved any problems, getting some surveillance set up both in the field and in that one pocket of the forest seems like the next logical step.

Shuri has just rounded the corner that'll put her at the back of the building when a figure steps out of an alley just ahead of her, but on the opposite side of the street. A man, she believes. Tall and thin and wearing an open tan trench coat with the high collar flipped up against the bite in the air. And though his sudden presence sends a very much *non-temperature*-related chill skittering from the top of Shuri's still perfectly styled head to the tips of her polished toes, she keeps her eyes forward. Pretends he's not there.

But then he crosses to her side.

And heads right in her direction.

"Don't panic," she says under her breath. Why had she thought it a good idea to roam a place she's never been, at night and alone?

As the distance between them shortens, she makes the decision to nod in greeting and keep it moving.

Five meters and closing fast (*sheesh*, this guy has long legs).

Three.

One—

"Good evening, Princess Shuri," he says in passing.

"Good eveni—"

Wait.

Shuri stops dead. And now can't breathe. Because she can see his shadow. And she knows that, whoever he is, he's coming around to face her.

She can't move. Not when the man stands at his full height in front of her. Not when she notices his charcoal-colored kufi and his dark sunglasses, or when he slowly reaches up to fold down his collar and she sees his ashen hands. Not even when he removes the sunglasses and she sees the bloodshot eyes and the cracked skin of his face. It's not nearly as pronounced as the woman in her vision/dream, but close enough for Shuri to have zero doubt that the man from the *Predator*'s security photos and the Wakanda-crushing woman are connected.

"Such a pleasure to make your acquaintance," he says in a deep rasp with a mocking bow of his head.

"You've been following us. Since we flew over you near the border. You can see my aircraft."

"Not exactly, no," he replies, clasping his hands in front of him. "But I have known precisely where you were during every minute of your journey."

But how?

Shuri's wheels spin, desperately seeking a viable course of action. She could run, but she knows he's likely to catch her. There are also no guarantees that he's alone.

The next option is an attempt to fight . . . though she hasn't trained in over a year—*thanks, Mother*—and swift movement will be difficult in this blasted dress. She wants to kick *herself* for wearing it.

"Who are you?" she asks, a feeble effort to keep him talking, though she has no idea what that will accomplish. Perhaps her trio of former Dogs of War will happen to turn the corner at just the right moment to come to her rescue.

"*Who* I am is of no consequence, Princess. The only thing that *truly* matters is what I plan to do."

"And what's that?" Shuri carefully, clandestinely shifts her feet into a fighting stance. Because she has a hunch about what his response will be.

"Well, to start, I intend to prevent your return to your beloved homeland." And with that, his hand shoots out quick as a flash, reaching for Shuri's throat.

16

A PANTHER
AND HER DORA

Shuri feels something like fire surge through her veins, and a lightning reel of recollections featuring T'Challa—of her days sparring and training—sparks through her mind quicker than a blink, igniting her muscle memory.

She uses her much shorter height to her advantage: ducking so that the man's hand closes around air, and then surging forward to plunge her bony shoulder into his unguarded midsection.

He stumbles backward, but with his unnaturally long arms is able to get a grip on Shuri's bicep as she tries to pull away. "Gotcha—"

The princess's left foot collides with his mouth as she twists beneath his arms and kicks her leg up behind her—*riiiiiiip!* goes the dress (oops)—escaping his grasp in the process.

As he folds at the waist, and his hands instinctively rise to his face, Shuri stands up fast, catching the underside of his chin with the thickest part of her skull to knock his head back, and then completing the blow with a full-force kick to his sternum.

He falls this time.

Shuri turns as fast as she can and attempts to make a run for it—

But the man manages to pin a piece of her ripped and dragging dress to the concrete with his foot.

She goes down hard, biting her tongue as her chin hits the pavement.

"Shuri . . ." She thinks she hears in a tinny, distant voice, but she must be imagining it. Her ears are ringing, and it takes a few seconds too long for her head and vision to clear: She's forcefully flipped from her stomach to her back and finds the man standing over her, lip busted and rage flickering in his dark pupils with every labored breath.

"You will regret your actions," he says. And he stretches down and grips the front of her dress in his fist to pull her to her feet . . .

But then one of his knees buckles, and he turns to look behind him.

Which gives Shuri just enough time to slip from his grasp and reverse roll to her feet.

She's upright just in time to see her rescuer land a roundhouse kick to the guy's jaw.

K'Marah.

A string of bloody drool flies from kufi-man's mouth as his head whips right.

"Eww!" the princess says.

It's the wrong move. He locks her in his livid gaze as he regains his balance, then lunges for her with hands outstretched.

Shuri yelps and manages to dodge so his grasping fingers close around air, but her feet tangle in her stupid, ragged-edged dress. Down she goes again, and this time, he doesn't waste a single moment. Her mouth opens, ready to scream, as he reaches to yank her to her feet—

But then his eyes go wide and surprised before they roll up in his head, and he collapses to the side with a thud.

Once he's out of the way, Shuri can see K'Marah

standing with both hands wrapped around what she recognizes as the thick, black marble panther figurine that was perched on the bookcase in Hunter's office. The mini-Dora's chest is heaving.

"Did he hurt you?" she says as she sets the stone cat aside to help pull Shuri to her feet. "Oh no, your chin!"

"I'm fine, I'm fine," the princess replies. "Thank you for coming to my rescue. Now let's tie him up before he comes to so he can't get away. Whoa . . ." She tries to stand up on her own, and her head swims.

"Cool it, sister," K'Marah says. "Here, you lean against the wall, and *I* will tie him up, *capisce?*"

"Ca-*what?*" Shuri replies, letting her head drop back against the brick.

"Ah, it's an old expression I learned from mid-twentieth-century white-American gangster movies."

"Of course you watch those," Shuri says with a roll of her eyes.

As K'Marah secures the man's hands and feet, woefully using strips of fabric from Shuri's ruined dress, Shuri uses her Kimoyo bracelet to call and let Hunter know the location of the trespasser. After a quick search of his pockets and person for evidence, weapons, etc. (they find nothing), K'Marah blindfolds him and ties a strip of fabric around his mouth as Hunter instructs. "You better be glad I didn't have my spear, you jerk!" she shouts into his unconscious face as she does so. Then the girls drag him into the shadows, leaving him there to be collected by Hunter's crew, before they scurry down the remainder of the block to the back entrance of the building as fast as their small feet will carry them.

Which isn't very fast. And both girls notice. "You *sure* you're not hurt?" K'Marah asks just as Shuri says, "You're not looking too hot . . ." They laugh, but Shuri knows it's more to break the tension than because something is funny.

"How'd you know I was in trouble?" Shuri can't help but ask once they're back in the parking garage, waiting for the elevator.

"I think you accidentally Kimoyo-called me." K'Marah lifts Shuri's wrist and holds it up to her own so they can both see the pair of illuminated beads. "I could hear the . . . scuffle. So I grabbed the first heavy thing I could find—and carry—and used our connected call to track you."

Track her. Hmm.

The elevator *dings*, and the girls step on the second the doors begin to slide open. As they ascend through the building, the weight of what just happened settles down around them. Shuri is *certain* there are a million-and-one questions lining up single-file on her friend's tongue, most of which she won't be able to answer. She braces herself as she hears the little intake of breath that lets her know K'Marah is about to speak.

But the other girl says only one word: "Tomorrow."

After getting cleaned up and changed, the girls decide—well, Shuri decides *for* them—that they'll sleep inside the *Predator* for the sake of making a swift exit as soon as they awaken. K'Marah replaces Hunter's panther figurine, and Shuri leaves a note on his desk to thank him and the others for their help and hospitality. Then utilizing the bead Lena gave her, which, as Shuri suspects, is akin to a master key for every high-security lock in the building, the girls retrace their steps to the landing pad—thanks entirely to K'Marah's flawless, Dora Milaje–trained sense of direction.

K'Marah, who really *wasn't* looking too hot, especially after the adrenaline subsided, is out like a pinched candlewick the moment she pulls the Vibranium blanket up over her shoulders and proclaims, "This blanket is the *best*." (Shuri knows it's going to disappear as soon as they arrive home.)

But try as Shuri might—even with her own delightful blanket—she is unable to sleep. And it's not even what she *knows* or has recently experienced that keeps her eyes wide and mind reeling. It's what she *doesn't* know: how the dry-skinned man has been keeping tabs on them.

With a huff, she climbs down from her bunk and goes to the *Predator*'s control panel, powering up both the electrical and navigation systems. While she knows that her Wakandan cohorts here in London surely have the technology to detect a flying object—including a soundless, invisible one with its radar turned off—she *must* figure out how kufi-man detected them on their way out of Wakanda.

Shuri programmed the detection alert mechanism to go off when one of two things happens: either something interacts with the *Predator*'s GPS signal, or it's physically spotted in flight—the latter of which is determined by tiny cameras all over the mirroring panels that track the focus of the eye, and can therefore "tell" when the vessel has been spotted.

Based on the security images, Shuri knows the latter set off the alarm just after they crossed the border.

But she's also fairly certain the man said he *couldn't* see the aircraft. ("Not exactly, no.") Is there a reason for him to have lied?

After running an overall avionics scan for glitches or bugs (there are none), Shuri scrolls through the signal log to trace all of the *Predator*'s digital interactions—with satellites, ground computers, etc. When nothing strange turns up there either, the princess runs an electronic scan of the cabin to see if there's a trackable signal lurking somewhere else on the aircraft.

A yellow dot lights up on the screen, and Shuri gasps.

There *is* a rogue signal.

And it's coming from K'Marah's bunk.

With the assistance of her Kimoyo bracelet and a few taps, the princess is able to reverse engineer the signal-acquiring mechanism in her Kimoyo card, turning it into a tracker-tracker that will pick up on any item that has been traced remotely. Then slowly, quietly, Shuri approaches her sleeping friend, waving the card over her blanketed body like a metal detector.

K'Marah is sleeping on her back with an arm draped across her face. And as soon as Shuri nears her head, the Kimoyo card lights up like a fiery flare.

She moves it closer to the pillow, and it dims. So she brings it back up over K'Marah's cheek. Signal's a bit stronger. Over her mouth, nose, eyes, onto her arm . . . brighter and brighter still until she gets to her wrist.

Which is when the card quietly *pings* and turns green.

K'Marah's fancy bracelet.

Odd.

Shuri carefully unclasps it from her friend's arm and carries it to the front of the *Predator* for examination.

Once there, she holds it up and shines her Kimoyo card flashlight over it. It certainly doesn't *look* out of the ordinary—for K'Marah the Glam, at least. The smoky-colored glass beads are cracked on the inside, which Shuri must admit creates a cool, sparkly-but-not-obnoxious effect. Though where someone would hide a tracking device . . .

She extinguishes the flashlight and sets the Kimoyo card aside. Then lays the bracelet across her palm.

The wave of lethargy that instantly crashes down over her is so intense, Shuri's knees buckle and she has to use the back of her captain's chair to keep from falling.

She forces herself back fully upright, gaze fixed on the unassuming piece of jewelry. Then, mustering strength she didn't realize she'd need, she uses the opposite hand to lift the bracelet so she's holding it in the air by the clasp like before.

Her sense of vitality returns. In fact, for the breadth of a few seconds, Shuri could swear she feels every cell of her body surge with life.

She raises her forearm to eye level and carefully lays the bracelet over her wrist.

Boom. Exhausted. And a bit nauseated this time, too. She picks it up . . .

And she's back to full force, even more awake and alert and *alive* than before.

Is *this* why K'Marah has been so tired and queasy?

"Wow!" She hears from behind her. "What time is it? Are we about to depart? Where is Queen Goddess Ororo-Storm?"

Shuri quickly stashes the bracelet behind her back as she whips around to face her friend. Her friend . . . who *looks* better. K'Marah's chin is high and her eyes are bright and her skin is glowing.

For a moment, Shuri can only stand and blink and stare.

"Why are you looking at me like that?" K'Marah says with a stretch. "Bast, I needed that rest. This is the most refreshed I've felt since we left home."

And that's all Shuri needs to hear.

"K'Marah," she says, going to sit beside the girl she realizes truly *is* her best friend. She holds the bracelet up, and K'Marah's eyebrows rise with it. "I think it's time we talk."

MISSION LOG

KEEPING THIS ONE SHORT BECAUSE WE NEED
TO DEPART, BUT I JUST HAD A CONVERSATION
WITH K'MARAH THAT WAS QUITE . . .
REVELATORY. IT WENT SOMETHING LIKE
THIS:

Me: Old friend, I'm not sure where
you got this bracelet, but it's
both being used to track us *and*
make you sick.

Her (staring at it, first in dis-
belief, and then . . . something
else): Oh.

Me: Do you remember where you
got it?

Her: (*silence* *avoidance* *refusal to meet my eyes*)

Me: K'Marah . . .

Her (sighing): You won't judge?

Me: Judge what?

Her: If you say "*I told you so,*" I will never speak to you again.

Me: K'Marah, what are you talking ab—

Her: Henny gave it to me.

Me: (*silence* *avoidance* *refusal to meet her eyes*)

Her: (*see line above*)

Me: I thought you said you've never met him in person?

Her (sighing again): I haven't. I . . . well, I told him I was going on a trip—

Me: K'MARAH!

Her: I know, I know. For what it's worth, I didn't mention *you*. But the package arrived by courier an hour later.

Me: So . . . he knows where you live, then?

Her: (*silence* *avoidance* *refusal to meet my eyes*) He must've . . . tracked my IP address.

Despite how quickly my mental cup ranneth over with questions—*Did you tell him of your training and career path? Our friendship? Your position as the Mining heiress? Was his goal to track you . . . or me?*—I said no more in the moment.

Because in spite of the questions, other pieces were clicking together in my mind. Like the existence of a (highly probable) relationship between this boy K'Marah thought was a friend, and the grown man who has been using the bracelet the boy gave K'Marah to follow us across two continents.

Though he can follow us no more—Hunter and crew delivered him to a maximum-security cell deep underground in the same building where Dr. Selvig's bizarre laboratory is located—I have the distinct suspicion that man was *not* out for the good of Wakanda.

Which would mean this boy K'Marah was communicating with likely does not have our nation's best interests at heart, either.

I managed to locate the bracelet's tracking mechanism and succeeded in reversing it. Now the next time someone attempts to pinpoint K'Marah's (our?) location, *we* will be alerted to *their* precise whereabouts.

I also succeeded in heating the bracelet beads to a pre-melt point that permitted me to collect a tiny bit of not only the coating but the glass itself. It is presently undergoing molecular analysis, and as soon as we are back in Wakanda, the result will upload to my database of chemical compounds for cross-referencing.

Ororo has just returned, so after I debrief her, we'll be on our way. I have no idea what awaits us back in our homeland and can only assume that T'Challa and Mother's silence is a result of all-consuming Challenge Day preparations.

At least that is my hope.

Any *other* reason no one seems to have noticed I'm gone . . . Well. I'd rather not think about it.

17

PREPARATION

One bright spot on Shuri's horizon: The polyelastane fibers accept a full-strength Vibranium infusion without disintegrating. The turnaround time will be tight, but provided they cross the Wakandan border by zero eight hundred hours and the fabric is waiting outside the entrance to her lab as she requested when she contacted the clothier, she should be able to get it infused and delivered to the clothier in time for him to work his sewing sorcery and have a habit prototype ready just before the Challenge.

Whether or not big bro will consent to wearing it for his ritual showdown is another question, but at least the princess has *something* semi-manageable to ponder over as they make their way back to Wakanda. Everything else might be crumbling, but T'Challa will soon have a moisture-wicking, kinetic energy–absorbing—and *storing* . . . and *expelling*—super-ultra-*STRETCHY* Panther Habit just like he asked for.

(She tries not to think about the fact that the perfect suit for T'Challa won't matter if he's bested.)

They part ways with Ororo three hundred kilometers north of Wakanda, shortly after Shuri begins their initial descent, and she exits the *Predator* with a look of fierce pride. But the closer they get to home, the more anxious the princess feels.

There are just so many unknowns. And the more she attempts to connect the dots, the less they seem connected at all. Ororo suggested Shuri inform T'Challa of the bits she does know, but the princess can't bring herself to do that because what exactly would she tell him? *"I got attacked by a man desperately in need of shea butter—who may be linked to a cracked-skinned woman I saw crushing Wakanda in a vision—after he tracked us using a bracelet that was delivered to K'Marah under the guise of being from a boy she met online who is supposedly a Jabari. OH, and I still haven't solved the herb problem, so they'll all be dead soon and you'll just have to stay Black Panther forever so PLEASE DON'T LOSE THE CHALLENGE! Here's a new suit, by the way!"*

It all sounds like nonsense.

And Shuri? Well, she feels like a failure.

Fifty kilometers north of the border, Shuri decreases the *Predator*'s speed and cranks up the rate of descent so that the girls can enter through the forest just like they exited: invisible, untraceable by radar, and utilizing Kimoyo tech to prevent signaling a border breach alarm.

And because she can't resist a peek at the area where they saw that encampment and were first "spotted" by their kufi-capped London assailant, Shuri makes a last-second decision to fly that way.

It's a decision she comes to appreciate . . . and regret.

"Uhhhh, Shuri?" K'Marah says from beside her.

"Yup."

"Not good . . ."

"Mm-hmm."

Because the girls can see that the small encampment a couple of kilometers beyond the Wakandan border with Niganda has grown. It's no longer a gathering of a handful of men with tents and campfires.

Now arrayed beneath them in perfectly formed lines is a certifiable army.

Shuri corrects course, heading northeast so they can cross the border a bit away from the impending invaders. As they cruise along the edge of the forest, Shuri taking full control of the vessel so she can turn at precisely the right angle for entry at a different point, K'Marah, who is standing with her forehead pressed against the front window, suddenly cries out: "Shuri! The forest!"

The princess peeks right and gasps. "Bast be with us . . ."

"Whoa!" K'Marah loses her footing as the *Predator* begins to tilt. "I know it's bad down there, Princess, but don't forget to drive!"

"Oh." Shuri rights the aircraft and tries to keep her breath steady as she faces back forward. But what she just saw is seared into her memory: a swath of dead trees like the ones she saw on the way out, and all around them, nonfunctional mechanized ones, the leaves of which are spotted that sickly yellow.

"It's spreading, Shuri!" K'Marah says, returning to her window post. "I can see it! More of the trees are dying!"

"Hold on tight! I'm turning around!"

Though it's risky flying *over* the greenery—and Shuri knows it will trigger the alarms in the capital—she also knows that a bird's-eye view will allow for the best scan of the trees so she can gather accurate information about how quickly they're being killed/disabled, and in which direction.

"K'Marah?"

The other girl turns.

"If we don't make it out of this alive, thank you for being my friend."

K'Marah rolls her eyes. "Save the drama for your mama, Princess."

It puts a temporary smile on Shuri's face as she accelerates just the slightest bit to push the *Predator* across the tree line and begin the terrain scan.

For a solid two seconds, Shuri thinks they're in the clear. But then the now too familiar alert rings out: *"Warning: This vessel has been detected."*

"Drat," from K'Marah.

"I can think of worse things to say," Shuri counters. "Let's just hope no one starts shooting or tries to over-take our navigation." She thinks of their friends in London. "Again."

The results of the scan pop up. "The security forest is deactivating by combination of organic death and mechanical failure at a rate of zero-point-three meters per second in the direction of the baobab plain. One thousand and sixty-two meters have already succumbed, and whatever is causing this shutdown appears to be creating a path approximately eight meters wide. As there are ten kilometers of forest between the border and the edge of the field, a way straight into Wakanda will be cleared in . . ." She taps around on the screen. "Eight hours, sixteen minutes, and thirty-three-ish seconds."

"Uhhh," is all K'Marah can say.

Not that it matters: Shuri is now clicking and swiping and tapping around on her Kimoyo card. "The Challenge is set to begin in"—*tap-click-swipe*—"eight hours, twenty minutes, and twenty-seven seconds." She shakes her head. "I really hate to admit it, but this was an exquisitely executed invasion plan."

K'Marah snorts.

"Hey, S.H.U.R.I.! Call T'Challa!" Shuri shouts into the air.

"Calling T'Challa," replies the same mechanically pleasant voice who just told them their very *detected* goose is cooked.

"Are you serious?" K'Marah says, flopping down in her seat.

"What? I have to tell him abou—"

"You named your AI after *you*? This is worse than the laboratory greeting!"

"It's an acronym! Stands for Super Heroics Universal Remote Interface . . ."

"Sure, it is—"

A hologram of T'Challa pops up in the center of the control panel. He's shirtless. "Shuri!" he says, clearly out of breath.

"T'Challa! There—"

"Well, *hello*, Your Majesty!" K'Marah says, looking at the hologram a bit more intently than Shuri is expressly comfortable with.

"Oh! Hello, future Dora! I am glad you two are safe—"

"T'Challa, where are you? We must speak to you at once!"

The hologram ducks, bobs, and throws a punch.

"Ooh!" K'Marah says, eyebrows lifting in delight.

The princess gags.

"Shuri, I can't—"

"*PLEASE*, T'Challa! It is urgent!"

"Stop, stop," he says to someone they can't see. Then he looks right at Shuri. "I'm at the Den. And as you've interrupted my training on *this* day, it better be."

When they step into the Den, the large, multistory facility where every warrior in Wakanda—from the border guards to the Dora Milaje—begins their respective training, Shuri gets smacked with a wave of nostalgia.

"Sheesh, I forgot how much it stinks in here," K'Marah says, getting hit with a different wave.

On the main level, where the youngest and newest trainees spend most of their time, there's a boxing ring for sparring, a sand pit for rod work, and a spring floor for acrobatics.

All three flood her with memories of Baba, and the days she was permitted to spend time here. "I miss this place," she says. *I miss him.*

But once they ascend to the third floor—the Special Forces wing—and Shuri sees her brother (with a shirt on now, thank Bast), she's back to business.

"T'Challa, there is an invasion mounting! At the Nigandan bord—"

"I know." And he takes a shockingly nonchalant drink of water.

"You *know*?"

"Of course I do." He walks past her and K'Marah to a table lined with various deadly weapons. Shuri sees three swords, one long and slightly curved, and two short; a variety of differently weighted spears (Shuri remembers him teaching her about the importance of weight); a set of nunchaku; an ax. He picks up a pair of daggers and turns back to face them, raising his arms. "I am the king."

K'Marah looks on the verge of fainting.

(*How vile*, Shuri thinks.)

"They are somehow creating a path in by neutralizing the security forest—"

"I am aware."

"—and they'll be able to break through, *right* at the field, five minutes before the Challenge begins!"

T'Challa sighs. He comes over and puts his hands on Shuri's shoulders and looks her right in the eye. "Shuri," he says. (Shuri tries to keep her breathing even despite the daggers sticking up on each side of her head, but she'll admit that it's difficult.) "Listen to yourself," he goes on. "You have interrupted the *king* of this nation, on the day that others will be permitted to challenge him for the throne and Panther mantle, because you think him unaware of the threat of invasion? At his own borders?"

Shuri gulps. "I—"

"While I can appreciate your zeal, Sister, it is clear that you are often lacking in both reason and foresight. I have known of this invasion threat for weeks now. And I can assure you"—now he smiles—"that it will not succeed. We are well prepared."

But Shuri's not ready to just . . . give up.

Because something still doesn't feel right.

"You are postponing the Challenge, then?" she says.

"Of course not." He moves away from her and into the center of a circle printed on the red rubbery floor. Begins to swoop and dip and jab with the daggers. "We will not shirk tradition for an easily routable threat."

"Well, what about the offensive?" Shuri says, already knowing the answer but unable to stop herself from asking. "Are you sending an army out to take them down?"

"Have they breached our borders, Shuri?"

"Well, no, but—"

"You, of all people, know that 'the offensive' is not our way." He does a spectacular flipping kick—knives in hand—and lands with his back to the princess. Then turns around. "Not that you *should* be privy to this information, but the moment our border is crossed, land and air troops are at the ready to thwart this so-called invasion before it can even begin."

Shuri clenches her fists, incensed. How dare he speak to her as though she knows nothing. As though the safety and security of Wakanda is not also HER highest priority—

Her Kimoyo bracelet buzzes, pulling her back to her senses. So she turns away from T'Challa and taps to reveal the message.

It's an alert from the *Predator*. A couple of Shuri's tests now have results.

Then a second alert pops up. This one even more jarring.

"K'Marah, we need to go," she says to her friend, grabbing her arm and pulling her toward the elevator.

Because while T'Challa might be *sure* the invasion won't be an issue, Shuri's not convinced.

Especially now.

"Molecular match," the first alert said.

Followed closely by *"Signal acquired."*

TO BE CONTINUED.

Photo by Rachel Moron

NIC STONE

is the *New York Times* bestselling author of the novels *Dear Martin* and *Odd One Out*. She was born and raised in a suburb of Atlanta, Georgia, and the only thing she loves more than an adventure is a good story about one. After graduating from Spelman College, she worked extensively in teen mentoring and lived in Israel for a few years before returning to the United States to write full-time. Having grown up with a wide range of cultures, religions, and backgrounds, she strives to bring diverse voices and stories into her work. Learn more at nicstone.info.

COLLECT THEM ALL!

Set of 4 Hardcover Books ISBN: 978-1-5321-4772-2

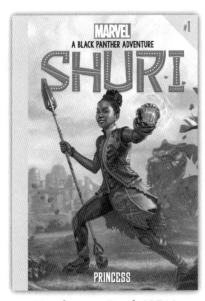

Hardcover Book ISBN
978-1-5321-4773-9

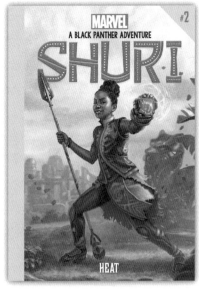

Hardcover Book ISBN
978-1-5321-4774-6

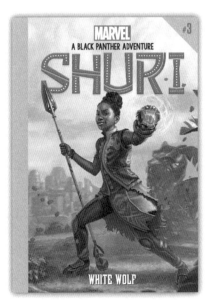

Hardcover Book ISBN
978-1-5321-4775-3

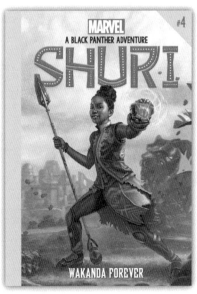

Hardcover Book ISBN
978-1-5321-4776-0